this book belongs to:
Este libro pertence a:

Come Bien Books
P.O. Box 19300
Oakland, CA 94619

First Edition
Printed in Malaysia

Furqan's First Flat Top / El Primer Corte de Mesita de Furqan
Written and illustrated by Robert Liu-Trujillo

Summary: A bilingual story about a boy, his first haircut,
and the trust built between father and son.

ISBN 978-0-9967178-0-9

Illustrations were created using watercolor, pen and ink on Canson Paper
Design by Joy Liu-Trujillo for Swash Design Studio

FURQANSFIRST.COM
COMEBIENBOOKS.COM

El Primer Corte de Mesita de FURQAN'S First Flat Top

Story & Illustrations
Cuento & Illustraciones
Robert Liu-Trujillo

Translation
Traducción
Cinthya Muñoz

Come Bien Books
Oakland, CA

Para mi hijo Saja Tushuna, gracias por tu sonrisa, tu risa, tu amor y todas las historias que has inspirado dentro de mi. No te olvides de siempre usar tu imaginación. Te amo.

– Papi

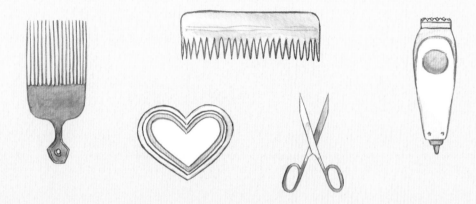

To my son Saja Tushuna, thank you for your smile, your laughter, your love and all the stories you have inspired in me. Don't forget to always use your imagination. I love you.

– Daddy

My name is Furqan Moreno. I'm 10 years old and I've always had real curly hair.

My Momma and Daddy let me grow my hair out
as long as I want; I just have to comb it.

But I decided I want to cut my hair a different way.

Mi nombre es Furqan Moreno. Tengo diez años
y siempre he tenido el pelo muy rizado.

Mi Mami y mi Papi me dejan que deje crecer a mi pelo lo más largo
que yo lo quiera; con la condición de que tengo que cepillarlo.

Pero he decidido que quiero cortar mi pelo de una manera diferente.

"Daddy?" I asked.
"Yes baby," said Daddy.
"Remember the way Marcus got his hair cut last year?"
Talking through toothpaste, Daddy mumbled "Yeah, that's called a flat top."
"I want to cut my hair like that. Can we go do that today?" I asked.

"¿Papi?" pregunte.
"Si amor," dijo Papi.
"¿Recuerdas la manera en que Marcus se cortó su pelo el año pasado?"
Hablando con su boca llena de pasta de dientes, Papi dijo, "Si, ese corte se llama
Corte de Mesita".
"¡Yo quiero cortar mi pelo así! ¿Podemos hacerlo hoy?" Le pregunte.

My Daddy said we could go so we took the number 14 bus
to Mr. Wallace's barbershop. It's the closest barbershop to our house.

Mi papi dijo que podíamos ir, así que tomamos el autobús numero 14
hacia la peluquería del Señor Wallace. Es la peluquería mas cerca a nuestra casa.

Once we got inside there's a whole bunch of people talking, things on the wall, the floor, the tables, and lots of people waiting to get their haircut. Maybe they were getting flat tops too.

Ya que entramos, había un montón de gente adentro platicando, cosas en la pared, el piso y las mesas y muchas personas esperando para que les cortaran su pelo. Tal vez van a hacerse un Corte de Mesita también.

When it was my turn I looked at all the stuff Mr. Wallace had.
He had all kinds of tools on his table.
Some of them for cutting hair.
And some, I couldn't tell what they were for.

Cuando era mi turno, miré todo lo que tenía el Señor Wallace.
El tenía todo tipo de herramientas en su mesa.
Unas eran para cortar el pelo.
Y otras, no podría decirte para que eran.

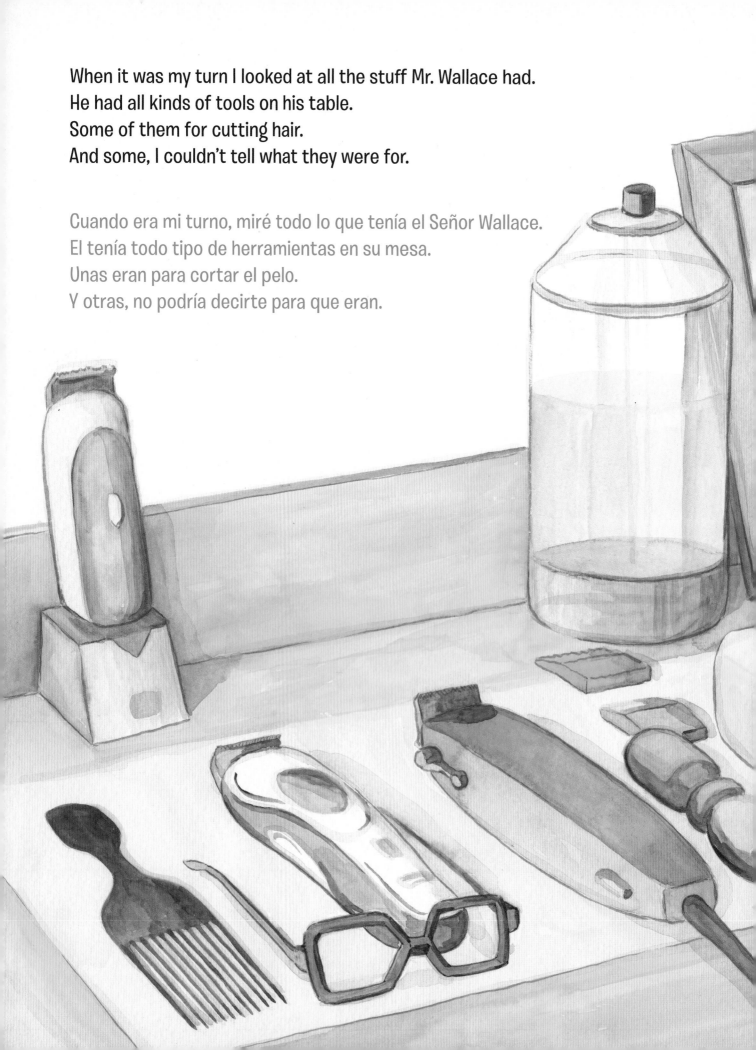

"I want to get a flat top!" I told Mr. Wallace.

But I was still a bit nervous about how to get it cut,
so I asked him to show me some pictures of people's hairstyles.

I pointed to the style I liked. As he began cutting,
I started to imagine how it would look.

"¡Quiero un Corte de Mesita!" le dijo al Señor Wallace.

Pero aun estaba un poco nervioso sobre como me lo debería de
cortar, así es que le pedí que me mostrara fotos de estilos de pelo
de otras personas.

Apunte al estilo que me gusto y mientras el empezó a cortar,
yo empecé a imaginarme como se vería.

Then I asked my dad, "Daddy!
But what if my hair comes out flat
like the drum Baba Shola plays in dance class?
Won't that look kind of weird?"

Entonces le pregunté a mi papi, "¡Papi!
¿Pero qué tal si mi pelo sale plano
como el tambor que Baba Shola toca en la clase de baile?
¿Que no se vería un poco raro?"

"Furqan, don't we both love the way
your teacher's drum sounds?
It will look cool, trust me,"
Daddy said nodding his head.

"¿Furqan, que no ambos amamos la manera
en que suena el tambor de tu maestro?
Se va a ver chido, confía en mi,"
Papi me dice asintiendo con la cabeza.

"But what if my hair looks flat like the pancakes
  we had for breakfast this morning dad?" I pleaded.

"Ahh", my dad said waving his hand.

"Pancakes are great, and yes they're flat.
  But your hair won't look or smell like pancakes boy!"

"¿Pero, que tal si mi cabello se ve como los panqueques que
  tuvimos esta mañana para el desayuno?" le pregunte suplicando.

"Ay," dijo mi papa agitando la mano.

"Los panqueques son estupendos, y si son muy planos.
  ¡Pero tu pelo no va a verse ni a oler como panqueques chico!

"At abuelita's house on Saturdays we make
    tortillas flat with our hands," I said.

Dad whispered, "Mmmm, tortillas."

"Will my hair look flat like that?" I asked.

"Tortillas are yummy, but no it won't,"
my dad responded.

"En la casa de abuelita, los sábados hacemos
    tortillas planas con nuestras manos." Yo dije.

Papá susurró "mmmm, tortillas".

¿Mi pelo se vera así de plano?" Yo pregunte.

"Las tortillas son muy ricas,
    pero no se vera así,"
    mi papá me respondió.

"Daddy remember that time
we tried to bake a cake?

"¡Papi! ¿Recuerdas la vez
que tratamos de hornear un pastel?"

It started out all puffy. Then it got flat.
Will that happen to my hair?" I asked.

"No baby, it will look better than that.
It will look real fresh. *Trust me,*" Daddy said.

"Comenzó todo infladito. Después se hizo plano.
¿Le pasará eso a mi pelo?" le pregunte.

"No bebe, se vera mejor que eso.
Se vera fresco. *Confía en mi.*" Dijo Papi.

"Ok, well what if it looks flat like cousin Mary's skateboard?
I don't want anyone stepping on *my* head," I said.

"I guess her skateboard is almost flat, but she's always
moving and laughing just like you. Don't worry," said Daddy.

"Muy bien, pero que tal si se ve igual de plano como la patineta de mi prima Mary?
No quiero que nadie se suba en *mi* cabeza," le dije.

"Creo que su patineta es mucho más plana, pero ella siempre
se esta moviendo y riendose igual que tu. No te preocupes," dijo Papi.

"You know how when you put
them records on the machine? I asked.

"You mean the turntable?" asked Daddy.

"Yeah, what if my head looks flat
like a record?" I said.

"¿Sabes, como cuando pones
los discos en la máquina?" le pregunte.

"¿Tu quieres decir el tocadiscos?" preguntó Papi.

"¿Si, que tal si mi cabeza se ve plana
como un disco?" pregunte.

"Your head would have to be pretty
big to look like a record boy.
It will look just fine,"
Daddy reassured me.

"Tu cabeza tendría que ser bastante
grande para verse como
un disco, chico.
Se va a ver bien,"
Papi me aseguro.

While I was thinking of flat stuff,
the barber almost finished cutting my hair.

It felt kind of funny when I leaned forward
or turned my head.

Mientras yo estaba pensando en cosas planas,
el peluquero casi terminaba cortando mi pelo.

Se sentía un poco chistoso cuando inclinaba
o volteaba mi cabeza.

Mr. Wallace asked if I wanted
designs like the Shakur twins had.

I told him "YEAH!" so he made all kinds
of patterns and then said...

El Señor Wallace me preguntó si quería
diseños en mi pelo como los que tenían los gemelos Shakur.

Le dije "¡SI!" así que el me hizo todo tipo
de patrones y después, me dijo...

"Your first flat top is done Furqan!"

I looked in the mirror, smiled, and
threw my hand up like I won a contest
because *it does look fresh!*

"¡Tu primer Corte de Mesita ya esta Furqan!"

Me mire en el espejo, sonrió, y
alzó mi mano hacia arriba como si gane
un concurso porque *si se ve fresco*.

The next day when I got to school
my friends were so surprised at my new haircut.

Some kids even looked at me funny, but mostly everybody liked it.

Al día siguiente cuando llegue a la escuela
mis amig@s estaban tan sorprendidos con mi nuevo corte de pelo.

Algun@s chic@s hasta me vieron medio chistoso, pero a la mayoría les gusto.

I told Daddy about my first day back at school
and he said, "I told you it would look good, didn't I?"

I thanked my dad again for taking me to cut
my hair different, and that is how I got my first flat top.

Le platique a Papi sobre mi primer día de regreso a la escuela
y el dijo "¿Te dije que se vería chido que no?"

Le agradecí a mi papi de nuevo por haberme llevado a cortar
mi pelo diferente, y así es como tuve mi primer Corte de Mesita.

Author's Note

When I think of all the work that went into this book I'm elated to finally share it with you. All the effort it took to get over myself, stop talking about it, and actually do it is a personal milestone. You are holding a story from the heart and a testament to the human spirit. Not just because I was able to write or draw it, but because you see it. You supported it. And I could not be more grateful. Over 276 supporters helped bring this project to life.

I used personal, observed, learned, and shared experience to craft this story. I hope it will serve as a mirror for you and your little ones to see a beautiful reflection of your life. I hope it will also be a window to see into a world you might not yet be acquainted with. It is important to me that this book be bilingual so that the two worlds can better understand each other and for cross cultural learning to begin. It is also very important to express pride in black hair. Furqan is an Afro Latino boy and I believe it is important for him and other children to see their hair as a positive aspect of their life.

Nota del Autor

Cuando pienso en todo el trabajo que entró en este libro, me siento exaltado de finalmente compartirlo con ustedes. Es un logro muy grande para mi el poder haber hecho el esfuerzo de hacerme a un lado de mi mismo, dejar de solo hablar al respecto y hacerlo. En sus manos tienen una historia que salió del corazón y un testamento al espíritu humano. No solo porque pude escribirlo o dibujarlo, pero porque ustedes lo ven. Ustedes lo apoyaron. No pudiera estar mas agradecido. Mas de 276 personas ayudaron para dar vida a este proyecto.

Use experiencia personal, observada, aprendida y compartida para crear esta historia. Espero y sirva como un espejo para ustedes y sus pequeñit@s para ver un reflejo hermoso de sus vidas. Espero y también será una ventana hacia el mundo con el que aún no están tan familiarizados. Es importante para mi que este libro sea bilingüe para que los dos mundos puedan entenderse mutuamente y para que el aprendizaje entre dos culturas pueda comenzar. También es muy importante el expresar orgullo en el pelo afro-descendiente. Furqan es un niño Afro Latino y yo creo que es importante para él y otr@s niñ@s el ver su cabello como un aspecto positivo en sus vidas.

Thank You

An immense thank you to my wife Joy. Thank you for your gentle push, kicks in the butt, support, creative direction, design, and encouragement through this process. I could not have finished this story with out you. We did it!

Thanks to the family and friends who helped spread the word: Mom & Gary, Dad, Raymond Jr. Wallace, Nicole Novela Martinez, Baba Qa'id, Brett Cook, MLA parents, TYS Collective, DOA Crew, Rolando Brown, Talia Taylor, Melanie Cervantes, Mia Birdsong, Vanessa Warren, Rad Dad, Colorlines, Hyphen, Chapter 510, Kickstarter Staff, Bad Girl Confidence, I Am the Nu Black, Bevel Code, In Culture Parent, Latin@s in Kid Lit, GhettoManga, 7 Impossible Things Before Breakfast, Kiss My Black Ads, Healthy Black Men, Utne Reader, Cane Row Kids, and the Black Science Fiction Society.

Thank you to my Bay Area Independent Children's book family: Janine Macbeth, Maya & Matthew Smith Gonzalez, Innosanto Nagara, Melissa Reyes, Aliona Gibson, Jill Guerra, Laurin Mayeno, and Malia Connor for

Photo by Tiffany Eng

helping me give birth to this story with your love & support. Can't wait to see more stories and grow our movement. Big thank you to Cinthya Muñoz for your patience, attention to detail and tone, persistence, and heart – and for your excellent work translating this story.

Big thanks to my mentors in storytelling who guided me on this long path in children's books: Gregory Christie, Ricardo Cortes, Doug Cunningham & Jason Noto, Maya Gonzalez, Simon Silva, Zetta Elliott, Mike Perry, Patt Cummings. Thanks for your guidance. Also, thanks to Duncan Tonatiuh and Shadra Strickland for your shining example.

This book was funded via Kickstarter with the help of over 276 people across the US (Bay Area to Brooklyn), Nigeria, Mexico, The Netherlands, and the UK. This book would not have been possible without your support:

Oakland Terminal Art Gallery · LaTanya Smallwood · Rod Wallace

A Tribe Called sOLStarr* · Berlin & Lucy Lee · connor · Me-Linh Tran Jenkins · Melissa Brown · Mia Birdsong Natalia Lopez-Whitaker · Nicole Mendoza · Nicole Novela Martinez · Paula Schwanenflugel · Qa'id, Marly, & Sekani Obatare · Rolando Brown · Roseann Vanessa Warren · Sarah Ball · Scott La Rockwell · Stephen Hassett · Tina and Ezra · Vincent Pan

Aaron and Yukari Baloney · Abigail Licad · Afrolicious · Aida Fei Wang Ross · Alfonso Hooker · Allison Crabb · amanda lopez · Amanda Wake · Amanda Yee · Amy · Andrea Wise · Anne Nguyen · Annie Auzenne · Anthony Carpenter · April V. Walters · Ashley Carr · astrid campos · B. Chavez · benjamin o rojas · Boutrose Saba-Norton · Brett · Brooke Ginnard · bryant terry · Burgos Family · C. Ellis · Cece Carpio · Chris Backas · Christ sidle · Christina Herd · Christina Santi · Christine Banks · Claudia Miller · Claudia Peña · Colin Masashi Ehara · Coriander · Craig Elliott · D. Henderson Dan Wolf · Dari · Darron Reese · Dawn D Valadez · Deborah Jesse · Desiree Hemphill-Davis · Dion Reiner-Guzman Dreamer · Élida Margarita Bautista · Elizabeth Ames Staudt · Ellen Choy · Ellen Dunn · Erica and Family · Erin Aults Erin Yoshi · Esperanza Navarro · Evangeline Reyes · Familia Pedraza-Palominos · Francesca Di Berardino · Fredman Family · Gabrielle Smith · Gina · GracesHomemade.com · Gus and Milo · Halline Haylow Overby · Hannah · Harper Masino · Hugo Giraud Jr. · Hunter Knight · Huong and John Nguyen-Yap · Indelisa Carrillo · Innosanto Nagara · Iyari Jasmine and Juan Julian · James Schoster · Jamila Rowser · Janine Macbeth & Family · Jay Gee · Jemar "Meezy" Souza · Jen Johnson · Jenabi Pareja · Jennifer Ortiz · Jessica Lopez-Tello · Jill Guerra Burger · Jill S. Thomsen Jim Cartwright · Jon Yang · jordan thurston · Josah Perley · Juana Alicia · Judy Gallian · Juliet Safier · KalaLea Sunshine · Kamal Kamara · Kari Koch · Kate Goka · Katherine Leung · Kathryn Schmidt · katie wolf · Kaya, Ade and Khalil Pearson · Keenzia Wilde-Budd · Kenya E. Davis · Khadijah Eid Mohammad Eid · Kim and Anisha Salazar Kim Bullard · Kiyoshi Ikeda · Kristin Zenee Black · Kristy D. Brehm · Kurrie · Kyla Portugal · L & L & L · Lady SoulFly Laurie L Young · Laurin Mayeno · Lawrence Guzman · LeSean Thomas · Libertad Rivera · Lucia Whitman · Maestra Nessa · Maggie · Martin · Mel · Melanie Cervantes · Melissa Reyes · Michael & Ryan Austin · Michael Z. Freedman Mikasa Curiosa · Mike Soe · Mlra Yusef · Miriam Klein Stahl · Mommy of Dragon · Momo, Thay-Thay, Lulu · Mónica Márquez · Morgan Pualani · Nadia Williams · Nancy Pili · Nick James · Nicole · Nicole Wong · Nora Berenstain Norris Family · Vicky Faulk · Oakland Public Library · Olivia · Omotara James · Oree Originol · OSAAT Entertainment P. Chang · Paloma B. Concordia · Pamela Zwehl-Burke · Patricia Augsburger · Perry · R. Gregory Christie · René Peña-Govea · Rhonda Ross · Ricardo Cortés · Richard Damien Comeaux · Robin Taylor · Roseli Ilano + Jacob Goolkasian Roy Miles Jr. · Sara Fewer · Shadi Rahimi · Shamilla Byron · Sharon · Sharon McKellar · Shiree M. Dyson · Shola Ajayi Simon, Sonia, and Lucien · Sincere Justice Allah · Sonia Lopez · Stephanie · SunHyung Lee · Susan Miller · Suzie & family · Taylor Neaman · Terry Park · The Aki family · The Faulring-Jonas family · The Hammers · The Mascarenhas-Swan family · The Portela Family · Theresa Ronquillo · Tom Jackson · tommy wong · Tricia Ong · Trish Broome Umala Mitchell · Valerie Titus-Glover · Verónica · Virak Saroeun · weysouth · Xylona Benton · Zai and Sky, Maya, Matthew Smith-Gonzalez · Zetta Elliott · Zoe

@redcowrise · Abby Phyfe · Alexander · Alvin Irby · Amanda Click · Angela Ferraguto · Beth Kasner · Callie Mackenzie Campbell · Chelsea Mangold · Chris Walker Christina R Quiroz · Danielle Albright · Dave Haylett · David J. Castillo · David Maggard · Dorena Banks · Elaine Stone · Eliza Stokes · Emma Gallo-Chasanoff · Erin Zipper · Fiona Nicholls · Grace Langshaw · Jenny Lee · Jesse Byrd Jr. · Joanna Eng · Jonaral Martin · Kate Andrew · Kathleen Gutierrez · Kelsey Wade · Kyle Knobel Legends of Enlightenment · Lorre Jacobs Daniel · Marzia · micah · Michele West · Monica M. Garcia · Nick Wulf · R.O.S.E. clothing · Rachel Anicetti · Robin DeRosa Sage Morgan-Hubbard · Salomeh Ghorban · Shelby-Lynn Dunkel · Stephanie Pereira · Stinky Robots · Sulaf Al-Saif · Terry Braye · Tiffany Eng · Victoria Rogers

Thank you

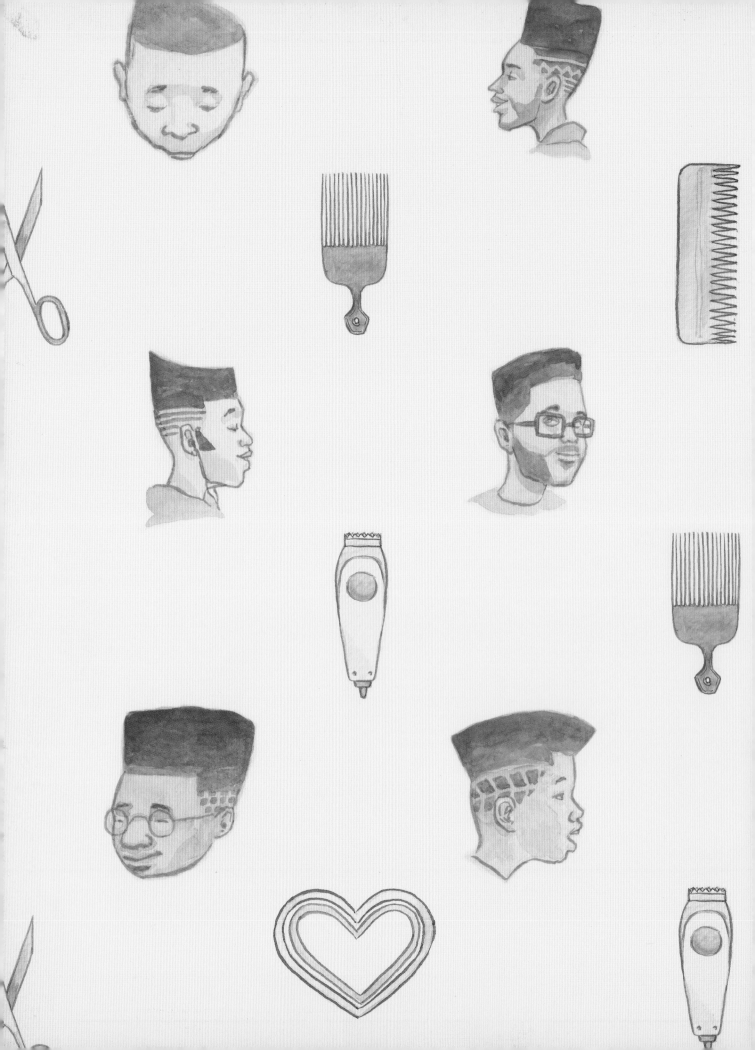